Dirty Bertie
BURP!

DAVID ROBERTS WRITTEN BY ALAN MACDONALD

stripes

JF

Dirty Bertie
BURP!

For Henry, who seems to have picked
up some of Bertie's dirty habits
(apologies to the hamster) ~ D R

STRIPES PUBLISHING
An imprint of Magi Publications
I The Coda Centre, 189 Munster Road,
London SW6 6AW

A paperback original
First published in Great Britain in 2007

Characters created by David Roberts
Text copyright © Alan MacDonald, 2007
Illustrations copyright © David Roberts, 2007

ISBN-13: 978-1-84715-023-3

Printed and bound in Belgium by Proost

10 9 8 7 6 5 4 3

Contents

CHAPTER 1

Bertie was the only one in his class who
actually liked school dinners. Lumpy
mash with gloopy gravy. Wormy spaghetti
with meatballs. Cold custard with slimy
skin on top. Bertie loved them all.

"Ugh! I don't know how you can eat
it!" said Darren at lunch on Friday. Bertie
slurped his rice pudding and gave an

extremely satisfied burp.

"Aren't you going to finish yours?"

"No," said Darren. "It looks like frogspawn."

"Pass it over," said Bertie.

Just then Miss Skinner, the Head, swept into the dining hall with a woman in a white coat. Miss Skinner rapped on a table to get their attention. "I want you all to meet Miss Beansprout, who is our new Head Dinner Lady," she said. "Miss Beansprout has lots of splendid ideas to improve our school meals."

Dirty Bertie

Miss Beansprout gazed at them fondly. "Children," she said, "it's my job to make sure you all have a healthy, wholesome diet. Who can tell me something that is healthy and delicious?"

Pamela raised her hand. "An orange," she said.

"Very good," beamed Miss Beansprout.

"An avocado," said Know-All Nick, showing off.

"Excellent," said Miss Beansprout.

"Nuts," said Bertie.

"Wonderful. Nuts are very good for you," nodded Miss Beansprout.

"Great," said Bertie. "Will we be having doughnuts tomorrow?"

"Stop talking and get on with your dinner," snapped Miss Beansprout.

On Monday Mrs Mould wasn't serving dinners behind the hatch as usual. In her place was Miss Beansprout. She had written a menu on the board.

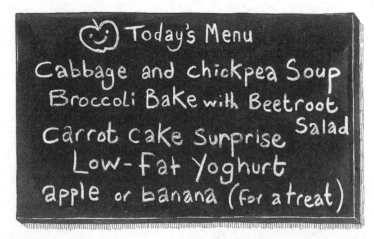

Today's Menu
Cabbage and chickpea Soup
Broccoli Bake with Beetroot Salad
Carrot cake Surprise
Low-fat Yoghurt
apple or banana (for a treat)

Dirty Bertie

Bertie and his friends stared in horror. Surely this was some kind of joke? *Broccoli? Cabbage?* Was she trying to KILL them?

"What's this?" asked Bertie.

"Lots of lovely fruit and vegetables," said Miss Beansprout. "Just what growing children need."

"But where are the chips?" asked Bertie.

"No greasy chips," said Miss Beansprout.

"Where is the custard?"

"No horrible custard."

"Where's the jam roly-poly pudding?"

"No stodgy puddings full of nasty sugar," said Miss Beansprout. "From now on we're all going to be eating delicious greens and nourishing salads."

"I love salad," said Know-All Nick. "A big helping for me!"

Dirty Bertie

Bertie gave him a withering look.

"Cabbage Soup or Broccoli Bake?" Miss Beansprout asked him.

"Can't I just have pudding?" asked Bertie.

"Broccoli Bake it is," said Miss Beansprout. She ladled a gloopy green mess on to Bertie's plate. SPLAT!

Next to it went the salad, swimming in beetroot juice.

"Yoghurt or Carrot Cake Surprise?" asked Miss Beansprout.

"What's the surprise?" asked Bertie, hopefully.

"The carrots are organic. That means they're bursting with vitamins!" beamed Miss Beansprout.

Bertie carried his tray over to a table to sit down. "I can't eat this," he grumbled, staring at his plate.

"You haven't tasted it yet," said Know-All Nick.

"Quite right, Nicholas," said Miss Skinner, who was on dinner duty. "Perhaps some *fussy* children could learn from your example. Eat up, Bertie, it looks delicious!"

Dirty Bertie

Bertie raised a forkful of green gloop to his lips. Darren leaned over to whisper in his ear.

"Boiled bogeys with squashed slug salad."

Bertie set down his fork. Suddenly he didn't feel at all hungry.

CHAPTER 2

Miss Beansprout's dinners got worse.
On Tuesday they had Celery and Nut
Crumble. On Wednesday it was Liver
Casserole and Sprouts followed by
Stewed Prunes. Bertie couldn't take any
more. At break time he called an
emergency meeting in the playground.

"If I eat one more vegetable I'm going

to be sick," he groaned.

"So am I," said Eugene.

"I couldn't stop burping yesterday," said Darren. "Great big smelly burps!"

"I know, I was sitting next to you," moaned Donna.

"Well it's no good just grumbling, we've got to do something," said Bertie.

"We could kidnap Miss Beansprout and lock her in a dungeon," suggested Darren.

"Good idea," said Donna. "Except we haven't got a dungeon."

"Well I'm not putting up with it any longer," said Bertie. "They can't make us eat it."

"Can't they?" asked Eugene.

"No," said Bertie. "Not if we all refuse. Not if we all say we're going on strike."

Dirty Bertie

Eugene looked anxious. "Won't we get into trouble?"

"Listen," said Bertie. "We're not eating anything until they give us back our old dinners. Right?"

"Right," agreed the others. Even lumpy mash and gloopy gravy would be better than the sickly slop Miss Beansprout gave them.

At lunchtime Bertie joined the dinner queue.

"What would you like? Liver Casserole and Sprouts?" asked Miss Beansprout.

"No, thank you," said Bertie.

"A big slice of Spinach Pie?"

"No thanks," said Bertie. "I don't want anything."

"Nothing? Don't be silly. You have to eat," said Miss Beansprout.

Bertie shook his head firmly. "I'd rather go without."

"So would I," said Darren.

"And me," said Donna. She nudged Eugene.

"Oh, me too … please," said Eugene.

Dirty Bertie

Miss Beansprout sent for Miss Skinner.
"These children are refusing to eat their
dinner," she said.

"Which children?" said Miss Skinner.
The others all looked at Bertie.

"We're on strike," Bertie informed her.
"Till you bring back the old dinners."

Miss Skinner smiled a thin smile. "I see.
You don't want any dinner? Well that's
fine with me."

"Pardon?" said Bertie.

"It's fine. Go
without," said Miss
Skinner. "Off you go!"

Bertie and his friends trooped away with empty plates. They sat down at a table and watched the other children chewing and slurping their food.

"I'm hungry," moaned Darren.

"So am I," groaned Eugene.

"I'm starving! I could even eat a carrot," said Donna.

Eugene gazed over at Know-All Nick's plate. "Couldn't we just have pudding?"

"NO!" said Bertie. "We're on strike, remember? We're not eating until they give us back our old dinners."

"But I haven't had anything since breakfast," grumbled Darren. "If I don't eat soon I'll starve to death!"

"Huh!" said Bertie. "Well it would just serve them right if we did. Maybe it'd teach them a lesson."

Dirty Bertie

CHAPTER 3

SLAM! Bertie arrived home from school. His mum was in the kitchen talking on the phone.

"Yes," she said. "Don't worry, I'll speak to him. He's just come in now."

Bertie had the feeling it was time to make a swift exit. He ran upstairs.

"BERTIE!" yelled his mum. "Down here

now. I want a word with you."

Bertie shuffled into the kitchen.

"What's all this about not eating your school dinners?" demanded Mum.

"Oh," said Bertie. "That."

"Yes, that. I just had Miss Skinner on the phone and she sounds very cross."

"It's not my fault," said Bertie. "The dinners are horrible! They're full of vegetables."

"Vegetables are good for you."

"But Mum, they're making us eat broccoli. And beetroot! And carrots!"

"Good," said Mum. "It sounds very healthy."

"How can it be healthy when I feel ill just looking at it?" asked Bertie.

"Don't make such a fuss, Bertie. It's only a few carrots!"

Dirty Bertie

"But Mum…"

"No buts," said Mum. "Tomorrow you eat all your dinner."

Bertie sighed. "OK."

"Promise me," said Mum.

"I promise," said Bertie.

As he went upstairs he smiled to himself. He'd promised to eat his dinner – but he hadn't said what would be in it, had he?

Dirty Bertie

PEEP! Miss Skinner blew her whistle for the start of school. Bertie hurriedly stuffed something down his jumper and fell into line.

"What if she catches you?" hissed Darren.

"She won't," replied Bertie.

"No talking at the back!" yelled Miss Skinner. "In you go."

The line of children began to file past the Head, who watched them with narrowed eyes. Bertie kept his head down. Another few metres and he was home and dry. An arm shot out and barred his way. Uh oh.

"Bertie," said Miss Skinner.

"Yes, Miss?"

Dirty Bertie

"What's that lump under your jumper?"

"Lump, Miss? Nothing, Miss."

"Really?" Miss Skinner's finger prodded his jumper. It crackled and rustled.

"Hands up," ordered the Head Teacher.

"What?" said Bertie.

"You heard me, hands in the air."

Bertie raised both his hands. A bag of crisps fell out of his jumper. Then two more.

"Pockets," said Miss Skinner.

Bertie turned out his pockets. Some sweets and chocolate bars scattered at Miss Skinner's feet.

"You know the rules, Bertie," she said. "No crisps or sweets in school." The chocolate disappeared into her pocket.

Dirty Bertie

Dirty Bertie

Later that day, Bertie passed the staff room on his way to lunch. He heard raised voices inside. "Thank goodness we don't have to survive on school dinners," said Miss Boot.

"Yes, they really are unpleasant," replied Miss Skinner. "Have another piece."

Bertie opened the door a crack and peeped in.

Dirty Bertie

He could see his teachers eating something. It was a bar of chocolate. *His* bar of chocolate. Bertie gasped. Well this time they'd gone too far. Nobody stole Bertie's chocolate and got away with it.

In the dining room Bertie stared. All his friends were eating their dinner.

"I thought we were on strike," Bertie scowled.

"Sorry, Bertie. I've got to eat. My mum made me promise," replied Eugene.

"Mine too," said Darren.

"Never mind, at least we tried," sighed Donna.

Bertie didn't answer. He wasn't beaten yet. If only he could think of some way to get revenge. He stared at the sloppy cauliflower cheese on Eugene's plate…

"It looks disgusting," he said.

"Yeah," agreed Darren. "Like flies in custard."

"Worms in ice cream," said Donna.

"Maggot jelly," said Eugene.

Bertie's mouth fell open. Why hadn't he thought of it before? Miss Beansprout was always boasting that her meals were made with fresh ingredients… Well maybe he would add a few fresh ingredients of his own!

CHAPTER 4

Next day Bertie waited impatiently for break time.

BRIIING! The bell sounded and the class thundered out into the playground. Bertie doubled back and slipped across the dining hall to the kitchen. He pushed open the door to check the coast was clear. Miss Beansprout was humming to

herself at the sink in the back room. He
would have to move fast. Bertie tiptoed
over to the fridge and opened the door.

There on the top shelf was his target
– a large bowl full of green salad. Bertie
pulled out the tin he'd borrowed from
his dad's fishing bag and took off the lid.
Inside was a sea of fat wriggling grubs.

"Dinner time, boys!" he whispered.

Half an hour later, Miss Skinner sat down
to eat her lunch. She raised a forkful of
green salad to her mouth and began to
chew. Strange, she thought, today it
tasted rather odd – sort of salty and
squishy. She gazed down at her plate.

Something in the salad moved. It raised its head and wiggled around.

"ARGHHHHH!" screamed Miss Skinner. "MAGGOTS!"

Her plate smashed on the floor. She clutched at her throat. Maggots! And she had just swallowed a whole mouthful! She grabbed a jug of water and glugged it down.

"Miss Beansprout!" she screeched. The Head Dinner Lady came running.

Everywhere she looked children were yelling, screaming and spitting their food on the floor. What on earth was going on?

"Look!" thundered Miss Skinner pointing at her plate. "Look!"

"I … I don't understand," stammered Miss Beansprout. "The salad was fresh this morning."

"Fresh?" thundered Miss Skinner. "It's crawling with maggots! Are you trying to poison me?"

Dirty Bertie

"I'm sorry, Miss Skinner. It won't happen again."

"You're right, Miss Beansprout," fumed the Head. "It certainly won't."

The following Monday Bertie was back in the lunch queue once again. The board with today's healthy menu had vanished. There was no sign of Miss Beansprout. Mrs Mould was back behind the hatch in her grubby apron. Bertie couldn't wait. *No more yucky beetroot or boring broccoli,* he thought, *mash and gravy here I come!*

Mrs Mould slopped a pile of spaghetti on to his plate. Bertie stared. It was sticky, wriggling and wiggling.

Just like…

He clapped a hand over his mouth
and fled from the dining room.

"What's wrong with him?" asked
Eugene.

"Dunno," shrugged Darren. "I thought
he liked wormy spaghetti."

STINKY!

CHAPTER 1

Bertie was busy working on an
experiment in his bedroom. For weeks
now he had been collecting the
ingredients to make a stink bomb.

Bertie's Super-smelly STINKBOMB - Mark ①

1 lump of pongy cheese   1 sweaty football sock
4 rotten eggs   3 mouldy cabbage leaves
1 tin of dog food   ① Dog hairs - a good handful

Dirty Bertie

Slip! Slop! Bertie gave the ingredients a good stir with a pencil and sniffed the murky brown goo. *Not bad*, he thought.

It just needed a few more days to get really good and pongy. Bertie couldn't wait to try out his stink bomb at school. Maybe he could smuggle it into Miss Boot's desk? Or, better still, splat Know-All Nick on the way home from school. Whiffer padded over and poked his nose into the plastic pot.

"Uh uh. No, Whiffer," said Bertie. "It's not for eating."

'Bertie's. Do not open or you'll regret it'

Someone was coming. Bertie quickly slammed the lid on the pot and hid it in his bedside cupboard.

Dirty Bertie

Mum poked her head around the door. "Bertie, what are you doing?" she asked suspiciously.

"Nothing," said Bertie. "Just playing."

Mum sniffed the air. "What's that funny smell?"

"Smell? I can't smell anything."

"It's disgusting," said Mum. "It smells like a family of skunks!"

"Does it?" Bertie looked pleased. The stink bomb must be a real humdinger if you could smell it from inside a cupboard. Mum was sniffing round the room trying to detect where the nasty smell was coming from. Bertie knew he'd have to act quickly before she investigated the bedside cupboard.

"PHEW, WHIFFER! Was that you?" he said, holding his nose.

Whiffer wagged his tail.

"That dog," sighed Mum. She turned back to Bertie. "I thought I asked you to tidy your room."

"It *is* tidy," replied Bertie.

Mum gave him a withering look. "Bertie! There's rubbish everywhere!"

Bertie inspected his room. Everything was where it normally was. On the floor.

"I like it like this," he explained.

"Well, I don't and I need you to tidy it up," said Mum. "Suzy's having a friend for a sleepover tonight."

"Who?" asked Bertie.

Suzy appeared in the doorway. "Bella," she said.

Bertie groaned. Not Bossy Bella. Of all Suzy's friends she was the worst. She would be trying to boss him around all night.

"And they'll be sleeping in here," said Mum.

Bertie's mouth fell open. He felt sick, he felt dizzy. "HERE? In MY ROOM?" he said.

"Yes," said Mum. "Your room's much bigger than Suzy's. We can put up the Z bed."

"But … but where am I going to sleep?"

"In Suzy's room."

Dirty Bertie

"NO!" yelled Bertie.
"NO!" screamed Suzy.
"It's only for one
night," said
Mum.
"I can't sleep
in here. I'll catch
fleas!" grumbled Suzy.
"Nonsense. Bertie's
going to tidy up."

"Tidy up? It needs disinfecting!" said
Suzy. "And what's that horrible smell?"

Mum pointed at Whiffer. "He needs to
go back to the vet's."

CHAPTER 2

DING DONG! Bertie could hear voices downstairs. Bossy Bella had arrived.

"Hello, Bella!" said Mum brightly.

"Hello," replied Bella.

"Have a super time, pumpkin!" said Bella's mum, kissing her on the cheek. "I'll pick you up in the morning."

Mum shut the door.

"Well then, why don't you show Bella where she's sleeping, Suzy?"

Bella handed Suzy her suitcase and clumped upstairs after her.

They found Bertie on his bed reading a comic.

"Get out," said Suzy.

"You get out," said Bertie. "This is my room."

"Not tonight. Mum says we've got to sleep in here, remember?"

Bella scowled. She hated little brothers. If she had a little brother she would give him to a charity shop.

"I'm not sleeping in his bed," she pointed. "It smells."

"You're the one that smells," replied Bertie.

"You do."

"No, you do."

"No, you do."

"Ignore him," said Suzy. "Let's play princesses. You can be Princess Bella."

"Princess Smella, you mean," sniggered Bertie.

Bella yanked Bertie off the bed. She twisted his arm.

"OW!" cried Bertie. He gave her a shove. Bella stumbled and fell on to the Z bed. Twang! It collapsed.

"Waaaahhhh!" she howled.

Mum came running upstairs. "What's going on?" she demanded.

"Bertie hit me," whined Bella.

"Bertie!" said Mum, crossly.

"I didn't!" said Bertie. "She practically broke my arm!"

"It was him that started it," said Suzy. "He's spoiling our game."

"Bertie, go to your room!" ordered Mum.

"This is my room," said Bertie.

"I mean go to Suzy's room and stay there till supper."

Bertie stormed out. It wasn't fair. He'd get those sneaky girls for this.

Dirty Bertie

"Supper time!" called Mum.

Bertie bounded downstairs. He was starving. He'd been in Suzy's room for hours and there was nothing to play with. Not even a pirate cutlass or water pistol. In the kitchen he could smell pizza and chips.

"Yum," said Bertie, helping himself to a large slice of pizza.

"Manners, Bertie!" said Mum.

"Yes, Bertie," said Suzy. "We always serve guests first."

Bertie reluctantly put the pizza back and pushed the plate under Bella's nose. Bella pulled a face. "I don't like pizza."

"Oh dear, never mind, have some salad," said Mum.

Dirty Bertie

"I don't like salad," grumbled Bella.

"Then just eat the chips," sighed Mum, piling some on Bella's plate.

"I don't like these chips. They're not like my mum's," complained Bella.

"Great, all the more for me!" said Bertie, reaching over to grab Bella's plate.

"Bertie!" snapped Dad.

Bella grabbed her plate and held on. Bertie pulled. Bella pulled back. The chips

catapulted into the air and landed on the floor.

Bertie bent down. He picked up a chip, wiped it on his shirt and ate it.

"BERTIE!" yelled Mum.

"What did I do now?" asked Bertie with his mouth full.

"Get down from the table and go to your room!" ordered Mum.

Bella looked at Suzy. They both smiled.

CHAPTER 3

After supper the girls sat down to watch
TV. Bertie burst in and threw himself
into an armchair. "Where's the remote?
Alien Arthur is on!" he said.

"We're watching the other side," said
Suzy. "It's *Make Me a Pop Princess*."

"What?" gasped Bertie. "But I always
watch *Alien Arthur* on Saturdays."

Dirty Bertie

"Let's take a vote," said Suzy. "Who wants Bertie's programme?"

Bertie put up his hand.

"Who wants to watch *Pop Princess?*" Suzy and Bella both raised their hands.

"Two votes to one, you lose," sneered Bella.

Bertie slumped in his chair, miserably. This was turning out to be the worst Saturday ever. And it was all the fault of Suzy and her bossy friend. He couldn't even go up to his room to work on his stink bomb because Mum said he had to keep out. Well, he wasn't going to be beaten that easily. There was no way he was sleeping in Suzy's bedroom tonight. Her walls were covered in posters of ponies and drippy pop stars. It was enough to give anyone nightmares!

Nightmares – that wasn't such a bad idea. Bertie slipped out of the room. A cunning plan had started to form in his head.

Thump, thump, thump! Bertie was banging on the bathroom door.

Bella opened up. "What?"

"I need the toilet. You've been in there hours!" complained Bertie.

Bella came out of the bathroom and barged past him.

"Goodnight, Bella!" said Bertie sweetly.

"Huh," she grunted.

Dirty Bertie

"I hope you can sleep," said Bertie.

Bella stopped. She turned round. "Why shouldn't I sleep?"

"You mean Suzy didn't tell you?"

"Tell me what?" said Bella.

Bertie lowered his voice.

"That my room's haunted."

"Ha ha, very funny," said Bella.

"Why do you think I've been begging to sleep in Suzy's room?" said Bertie.

"You didn't beg, your mum made you."

Bertie shook his head. He glanced around. "It's the noises," he whispered. "They keep me awake."

"Noises?" said Bella.

"The bumps and thumps. The moans and groans," said Bertie.

"Oh," said Bella, turning rather pale.

"Still, some people don't hear them.
It's only if you're scared of ghosts. You're
not, are you?"

"Me?" said Bella. "Course not."

"That's OK then. Sweet dreams!"

Bertie closed his door and smiled to
himself. *That ought to do it*, he thought.

Eleven o'clock. Bella was tossing and
turning in her bed. She couldn't sleep.

Her mattress was too lumpy. The room was too dark. Worst of all, she kept imagining she heard strange noises. Of course Bertie had been making it up. Suzy said he was. There was no such thing as ghosts.

CREAK, CREAK, CREAK!

What was that? Bella held her breath.

THUMP, THUMP, THUMP!

It sounded like footsteps on the landing. Bella gripped the covers tightly.

"Suzy?" she hissed. "Suzy. Are you awake?"

There was no answer from the Z bed.

RATTLE, RATTLE! went the door handle.

"EEEEEEEEEHHH!" went the door as it swung open by itself.

"Help!" whimpered Bella, diving under the covers. "Who's there?"

Dirty Bertie

She peeped out. There it was! A ghost
stumbling through the dark towards her.

"Wooooooooh!" it moaned.
"Wooooooooh!"

"Suzy," croaked Bella. "Suzy, wake up!"

"Wooooooooooh," moaned the ghost.

Closer and closer it came. Bella could

see its bare white feet.

"You must leave this place!" it moaned.
"Leave this … OUCH!"

A pillow had thwacked the ghost on
the back of the head. Suzy yanked off
the ghost's white sheet, revealing its blue
pyjamas.

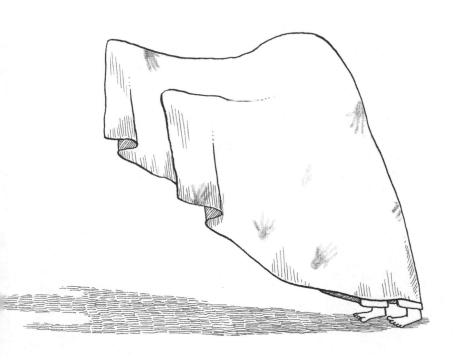

Dirty Bertie

"BERTIE!" snarled Suzy.

"Um, hello," said Bertie.

"Get out," said Suzy. "Get out and don't come back."

"Or what?" said Bertie.

WHUMP! A pillow whacked Bertie in the face. THUMP! Another clouted him on the ear. Bertie fled from the room under a hail of blows.

"And next time I'm telling Mum!" Suzy called after him.

Bertie shut the door behind him. Trust his rotten sister to wake up and spoil everything. He would have to try plan B.

Midnight. The house was as quiet as the grave. Suzy was asleep. Bossy Bella was asleep. Bertie was not asleep. He was creeping along the landing with something in his hand. He opened his bedroom door and stole inside. Now where to hide? His eyes fell on the windowsill above Bella's bed. Perfect! Bella was talking in her sleep. "Get off. It's my go," she mumbled.

Bertie peeped out from behind the curtains. He brought out a big plastic spider on a string. Slowly he began to lower the spider towards his victim. Lower and lower it dangled, spinning round on its string. Bertie leaned out a little further to get a better view. The spider brushed Bella's hair. Bella's eyes snapped open. They bulged with fear. A giant black tarantula was inches from her face. Its red eyes were staring at her. It waggled its eight hairy legs.

Dirty Bertie

"ARGGHHHHHHHH!" screamed Bella.

Bertie was so startled he slipped off the windowsill and landed on top of Bella, who kicked and screamed.

"ARGH! GEROFFME! HEEEELP!"

The noise woke up Suzy.

"Muuuuuuum! Bertie's in our room!"

CLICK! The bedroom light came on. Mum stood in the doorway wrapped in her dressing gown.

"Bertie!" she seethed. "What do you think you're doing?"

"There was a huge black spider!" wailed Bella. "It was in my hair!"

Mum bent down. She picked the plastic spider off the floor and dangled it under Bertie's nose.

"Yours, I think," she said.

"Oh, um, thanks. I was looking for

that," said Bertie.

Mum glared at him. "Go to your room. And if I catch you out of bed one more time there'll be no sweets for a month."

Bertie trooped back to his room. He closed the door behind him and got into bed. Operation Ghost had failed. So had Operation Spider. He thought he better not try Operation Ants in the Pants. It looked like he'd be sleeping in Suzy's bed tonight after all.

CHAPTER 4

Meanwhile, in Bertie's bedroom, Bella
was still awake. She wished Suzy's mum
hadn't mentioned sweets. Thinking of
sweets always made her hungry. She'd
practically had nothing at all for supper.

At home she always kept a stash of
sweets handy in case she got hungry at
bedtime. Maybe Suzy's horrible little

brother had some hidden somewhere?

Bella looked under the bed. Nothing there. She looked under the pillow. Nothing. She opened the bedside cupboard. On the shelf was a small plastic pot. Eagerly, Bella took it out and read the words scrawled on the side.

Ahaa! Sweeties! thought Bella.

She prised off the lid and peered inside.

A foul, putrid smell hit her like a force-ten gale. The pong of mouldy cabbage and rotten eggs filled the room. Bella clapped a hand to her mouth. She was going to be sick. She couldn't breathe.

"AHHHH! UGGGHHHHH!" she cried, dropping the stink bomb.

Suzy woke up.

"Bella! What are you … EURGH! What's that dreadful stink?" she gasped.

"I'm dying!" choked Bella. "I'm suffocating! Let me out!"

BANG! BANG! BANG!

Someone was hammering on Bertie's door.

Suzy and Bella burst in. "I need my bedroom back!" panted Suzy.

"What?" asked Bertie.

"It's horrible! It stinks! You've got to let us sleep in here!" begged Suzy.

"What are you talking about?"

"The smell — from that thing! It's choking us."

It dawned on Bertie — the stink bomb. He'd forgotten all about it.

"So you want me to give you back your bedroom?" he said slowly.

"Yes, yes. Please, Bertie! We can't sleep in there!" said Suzy.

"Hmmm," said Bertie. "I'll have to think about it."

"We'll do anything!" pleaded Bella.

Bertie raised his eyebrows. "Anything?"

Five minutes later Bertie was settled back in his own bed. True the room was a little whiffy, but he didn't really mind. Once you got used to it, the smell wasn't so bad — he couldn't see why the

girls were making such a fuss. In any case
all that mattered was he was back in his
own room. And tomorrow Suzy and
Bella had promised to play whatever he
wanted. Bertie had already thought of a
good game – it was called Pass the
Stink Bomb.

WALKIES!

CHAPTER 1

"Dog training classes?" Bertie stared at his mum in horror.

"Yes. No arguments, please, Bertie," said Mum.

"But why do I have to go?"

"Because someone has to take Whiffer. He can't go on his own."

"Why can't you take him?" asked Bertie.

"I'm far too busy."

"What about Dad then?"

"Oh no," said Dad hastily. "I'm *really* busy. Anyway he's your dog."

"But he doesn't need training!" protested Bertie.

Mum snorted. "Bertie! He barks every time the doorbell goes."

"And he's always climbing on the sofa," grumbled Dad.

"He licks food off your plate," said Mum. "And last week he did a poo on Mrs Nicely's lawn."

"He's a dog," said Bertie. "That's what dogs do!"

"Well it's high time he learned to behave," said Mum firmly. "And I'm told this dog trainer can work wonders."

Bertie sighed. It wasn't fair. He didn't

want to take Whiffer to training classes.
He got quite enough classes at school.

"Anyway, he *is* trained," he argued. "I've
been training him for ages."

"Bertie, he does what he likes," said
Mum.

"Not always," said Bertie. "Sometimes
he listens to me."

Mum gave him one of her looks.
Whiffer was dozing on his cushion in the
corner. Bertie turned to him and
pointed.

"Stay, Whiffer," he ordered. "STAY!"

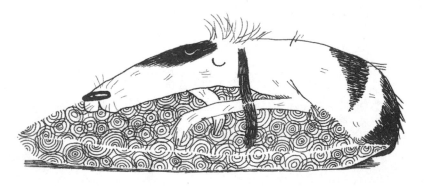

Whiffer opened one eye lazily then
went on dozing.

"See?" said Bertie. "Like I said – he
does what I say."

Mum folded her arms. "Very funny. You
are taking him to classes and that is the
end of it."

The following Friday evening Dad drove
Bertie and Whiffer to the leisure centre.

In the big hall dogs of all shapes and
sizes waited with their owners. Whiffer
pulled at his lead and whined. He
wanted to make friends.

The trainer was called Miss Bowser.
She had wiry hair and a face like a bad-
tempered bulldog. Bertie could see why
animals would obey her.

Dirty Bertie

Miss Bowser clapped her hands and told everyone to line up for inspection.

"Mmm," she said, patting a red setter. "Good, good. Splendid."

When she came to Whiffer she stopped and clicked her tongue.

"And what have we here?"

"My dog," said Bertie.

"I can see it's a dog. I mean what is his *name*?"

"He's called Whiffer."

"Whiffer?" she barked. "That's an odd name for a dog."

"Well he can be pretty smelly, especially when you're watching TV," explained Bertie. "Sometimes he does one and the pong's so bad you can smell it upstairs."

"Good gracious!" said Miss Bowser, drawing back a little.

Dirty Bertie

"I don't think he can help it," said
Bertie.

"He will LEARN to help it," Miss
Bowser replied, grimly. "In my classes
dogs do what they are told." She eyed
Whiffer and raised a stern finger.

"SIT!" she ordered.

Whiffer sat. Bertie was amazed. He'd
never done that for anyone before.

CHAPTER 2

The class began. Miss Bowser handed out dog biscuits.

"Treats must be earned," she told her class. "A naughty dog does not get a treat. Let's begin with a simple command. Teaching your dog to come when called."

Bertie groaned. He'd tried a million times

to get Whiffer to come. The only time he came was when his dog bowl was full.

"Step away from your dog and turn to face them," instructed Miss Bowser.

Bertie walked away from Whiffer. When he turned round, Whiffer was right behind him, wagging his tail. He could smell dog biscuits.

"No, Whiffer. You stay over there," said Bertie. "You come when I say 'Come', OK?"

Whiffer licked his hand and tried to nose in Bertie's pockets. Bertie dragged him back to his place by the collar.

"Now call your dog by name," said Miss Bowser. "When he comes give him a treat. And remember, heaps and heaps of praise."

"Whiffer! Come, boy!" called Bertie.

Whiffer looked the other way.

"Come, boy. Come! COME!" yelled Bertie.

Whiffer was the only dog in the hall who hadn't moved. The other owners cooed and fussed over their dogs, who were wolfing down their biscuits. Miss Bowser strode over to Bertie.

"Where is your treat?" she boomed.

"Um, in my pocket."

"No, no, you have to let him see it! Give it to me!"

Miss Bowser held out her hand with the dog biscuit. Whiffer barked and flew at her – a whirlwind of fur and legs and tongue.

Miss Bowser found herself pinned to the floor, with Whiffer on top of her, crunching his biscuit happily.

81

Dirty Bertie

"How did it go?" asked Mum when Bertie got home later that evening.

"It was terrible," groaned Bertie, slumping into a chair. "It's worse than school."

Whiffer padded over to his cushion and flopped down wearily.

"Never mind," said Mum. "It's only the first lesson. I'm sure it will get better."

"You haven't met Miss Bowser," said Bertie darkly. "She shouts all the time – even when she's standing right next to you. I bet she used to be in the army. I bet she got tired of shouting at soldiers all day and decided she'd get a job shouting at dogs and their owners."

"As long as Whiffer does what he's told I don't mind," said Mum.

Dirty Bertie

"That's just it, he doesn't!" moaned Bertie. "He gets mixed up. He sits when he's meant to come and when I say 'Walkies', he lies down! The only thing he's good at is stuffing himself with biscuits!"

Mum glanced at Whiffer, who had dozed off to sleep. "Well there's seven more weeks, he's bound to improve."

"Seven?" Bertie groaned. Seven more weeks of Miss Bowser shouting and Whiffer coming bottom of the class. He didn't know if he could stand it.

"And you didn't tell me there'd be a test," he grumbled. "Whiffer's got to pass his ODD."

"His what?" asked Mum.

"ODD. Obedient Dog Diploma," said

Bertie. "That's what she gives you."

"Good," said Mum. "With what it's costing me I'll expect him to pass."

Bertie looked doubtful. "Well," he said. "I wouldn't bet on it."

Mum had an idea. "How about this?" she said. "I'll offer you a reward. If Whiffer passes I will double your pocket money."

Bertie looked up. "Really?"

"Really."

Bertie did a quick calculation. Double pocket money that would be ... um ... double what he usually got, which came to quite a lot. He could buy loads of things with twice the pocket money.

There was just one major problem. There was more chance of Whiffer passing his *driving test* than his Dog Diploma.

CHAPTER 3

Every week for the next six weeks
Bertie dragged Whiffer along to Miss
Bowser's classes. Whiffer showed no
signs of progress. He made friends with
a boxer called Bonzo. He learned to
steal biscuits from Bertie's pocket. But
he didn't learn to obey. Bertie was in
despair. At school he explained the

problem to Donna. Donna had a hamster and a goldfish so she knew about pets. She suggested they take Whiffer to the park for extra lessons.

"It's no use," moaned Bertie, after Whiffer had gone charging off for the umpteenth time. "Let's face it, he's never going to pass."

"Maybe you're just doing it wrong," said Donna.

"How can I be? I'm shouting just like she does."

Whiffer came racing up. He'd found a mangy old rubber ball in the grass.

"Try one more time. Tell him to sit," said Donna.

"SIT!" yelled Bertie.

"WHIFFER, SIT!"

Dirty Bertie

Whiffer dropped the ball at Bertie's feet and barked. Bertie flopped down on the grass. Whiffer sat down too. Donna looked thoughtful.

"Let's try something else. I'll go over there and you come when I call you."

"Me?" said Bertie. "It's not me we're meant to be training!"

Donna looked at him. "Do you want my help or not?"

Bertie sighed. Donna could be very bossy when she wanted to be.

"Ready?" said Donna. "OK. Come!" Bertie walked over to her and Whiffer trotted behind. Donna looked pleased.

"Now roll over," she said.

"Who?"

"You! Go on, do it!"

Feeling pretty stupid, Bertie lay down

and rolled over. Whiffer barked joyfully and rolled over too. This was a great game.

"See! I was right," laughed Donna. "He does whatever you do. All you have to do is get him to copy you!"

"Wow!" said Bertie. "You're a genius!"

"I know," said Donna, modestly.

Bertie still looked worried. "But what about the test?" he asked. "It's not just rolling over, there'll be tunnels and fences and stuff."

"Easy!" shrugged Donna. "You just do it with him. Trust me. It'll work."

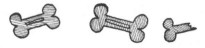

The following Friday Miss Bowser's class gathered for their final exam. Bertie eyed the other dogs – Bonzo the boxer, Trixie

the terrier and Dodie the Dalmatian.
They had all been washed and combed
for their big day.

Out in the park was a doggy obstacle
course. There were tiny hurdles, poles to
weave through and a long blue tunnel.
Miss Bowser had her clipboard and
pencil at the ready to mark each dog's
performance. Whiffer tugged at his lead.
Over on the other side of the park he'd
spotted some boys playing frisbee.
Frisbee was his favourite game.

Dodie was first to be tested. She
scored top marks, 10 out of 10 with
no refusals. Bertie
watched Bonzo
and Trixie complete
the course with
flying colours too.

Dirty Bertie

Whiffer didn't seem to be paying attention. He kept staring across the park.

Finally it was Bertie's turn. "OK, Whiffer," he whispered. "Just follow me." He set off at a run and cleared the first hurdle.

Miss Bowser waved her clipboard. "No, no, Bertie! The dog, not you!"

But Donna's plan was working. Whiffer copied Bertie, stepping over the hurdles and clearing the jump like a racehorse. Bertie got down on his hands and knees to crawl through the tunnel.

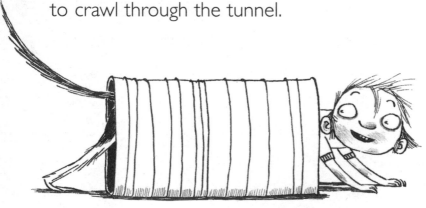

Dirty Bertie

He danced in and out of the poles as everyone watched in amazement. Almost there! Suddenly a red frisbee whizzed by and hit him on the head.

Whiffer barked excitedly. A frisbee meant a game. *Uh oh*, thought Bertie and grabbed it before Whiffer could pounce. A boy in a football shirt ran up.

"Hey! That's ours!" he said.

Bertie meant to throw it back, but like most frisbees this one had a mind of its own. It took off and curved back over his head. It zoomed over the line of waiting dogs like a low-flying jet. Fifteen pairs of eyes watched it go. Fifteen dogs barked and leaped in the air, straining at their leads. Whiffer saw the frisbee coming back his way. He leaped high, caught it in his mouth and set off like a

greyhound. Before you could shout
"Stay!" the other dogs were after him.

"Yikes!" cried Bertie, dodging out of
the way as the pack thundered past.
Dogs flattened Miss Bowser's hurdles.
Dogs swarmed like rats through the blue
tunnel. Miss Bowser tried to stop them.
She held up her hand like a policeman
stopping the traffic. "SIT!" she yelled.
Bonzo leaped at her and she vanished in
the scrum.

CHAPTER 4

It took some time for all the dogs to be rounded up. The frisbee was returned to its owners slightly chewed at the edges. The blue tunnel had somehow got ripped. But what Bertie didn't understand was why everyone blamed him!

"It wasn't my frisbee!" he pointed out.

"I could've been killed getting bashed on the head like that. Instead of blaming me, you should be asking if I'm all right!"

Miss Bowser did not seem to care if Bertie was all right. She had grass in her hair and muddy paw prints all over her skirt. She said they would get on with the awards so everyone could go home.

Bertie watched gloomily as each dog and his owner went forward. He doubted if Whiffer would be getting his Diploma, not after all the fuss there'd been.

"And finally…" said Miss Bowser. "Bertie and Whiffer."

Bertie trooped out to the front. Miss Bowser glared at him.

"In twenty years I have never met a dog I couldn't train," she said. "Until now." She lowered her voice. "However, I

will give you this on one condition. That
you promise you will never ever come
to one of my classes again."

"Oh, I won't," said Bertie. "Honestly."

"Very well," said Miss Bowser, handing
him a piece of paper.

Bertie looked at it.

> Obedient Dog Diploma.
> Class 1. Awarded to:
> Whiffer

"Wow! Thanks!" he said. "Look, Whiffer.
You passed!"

Ten minutes later Bertie ran over to
the car park where his mum was waiting.

"Look, Mum!" he cried. "We did it!
Whiffer passed!"

Mum was delighted. She handed
Bertie his pocket money – double his
usual amount. "Well done, Bertie. And

clever old Whiffer, I told you he could do it!" She glanced behind Bertie. "Where is he, by the way?"

Bertie looked round just in time to catch sight of Whiffer racing across the field. He called out to him.

"Whiffer! Here, boy! Come!"

Whiffer didn't even look back.

Obedient Dog Diploma.
Class 1. Awarded to:
Whiffer